My 1st Classic Story

The Little Red Hen

a retelling by Christianne C. Jones

illustrated by Natalie Magnuson

PICTURE WINDOW BOOKS

a capstone imprint

My First Classic Story is published by Picture Window Books
A Capstone Imprint
151 Good Counsel Drive, P.O. Box 669
Mankato, Minnesota 56002
www.capstonepub.com

Originally published by Picture Window Books, 2005.
Copyright © 2011 by Picture Window Books.
All rights reserved. No part of this publication may be
reproduced in whole or in part, or stored in a retrieval
system, or transmitted in any form or by any means,
electronic, mechanical, photocopying, recording, or
otherwise, without written permission of the publisher.

Library of Congress Cataloging-in-Publication Data
Jones, Christianne C.
The little red hen / retold by Christianne C. Jones ;
illustrated by Natalie Magnuson.
p. cm. — (My first classic story)
Summary: The little red hen finds none of the lazy barnyard
animals willing to help her plant, harvest, or grind wheat into
flour, but all are eager to eat the bread she makes from it.
ISBN 978-1-4048-6073-5 (library binding)
ISBN 978-1-4048-7356-8 (paperback)
[1. Folklore.] I. Magnuson, Natalie, ill. II. Title.
PZ8.1.J646Li 2011
398.2—dc22
[E]   2010003625

Art Director: Kay Fraser
Graphic Designer: Emily Harris

Printed in the United States of America in Stevens Point, Wisconsin.
062011   006273

The story of *The Little Red Hen* has been passed down for generations. There are many versions of the story. The following tale is a retelling of the original version. While the story has been cut for length and level, the basic elements of the classic tale remain.

The little red hen had a full house.

She lived with a cat, a dog, and a mouse.

The cat, the dog, and the mouse were a lazy bunch.

They slept all day while the little red
hen worked.

She did all of the cooking, cleaning, and gardening.

One day, while she was in the garden, the little red hen found some grains of wheat.

PEAS

CARROTS

BEANS

11

"Who will help me plant this wheat?"
she asked.

"Not I!" said the cat.

"Not I!" said the dog.

"Not I!" said the mouse.

"Then I guess I will do it myself," said
the little red hen.

So she planted the wheat and helped
it grow.

When the wheat was ready, the little red hen asked, "Who will help me cut this wheat?"

"Not I!" was all she heard.

"Then I guess I will do it myself!"
she exclaimed.

So the little red hen cut the wheat herself.

After the wheat was cut, the little red hen said, "This wheat must be ground into flour. Who will take it to the mill?"

Again she heard, "Not I!"

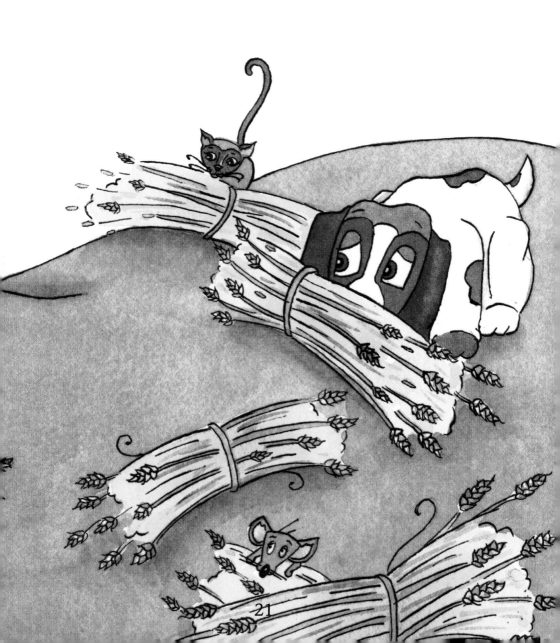

"Then I guess I will do it myself," she said with a sigh.

So the little red hen took the wheat to the mill. She returned with a big sack of flour.

"Who will help me make bread from this flour?" she asked.

"Not I!" shouted the cat.
"Not I!" shouted the dog.
"Not I!" shouted the mouse.

The little red hen muttered, "Then I guess I will do it myself."

She spent the entire afternoon baking bread.

When the bread was done, the little red hen asked, "Who will help me eat this bread?"

"I will!" yelled the cat.

"I will!" yelled the dog.

"I will!" yelled the mouse.

"I don't think so. I have done everything else myself. I will eat this bread myself, too," the little red hen said with a smile.

And she ate every last crumb all by herself.